NANA'S MAGIC BLANKET

Sandi Beech

AuthorHouse™ UK
1663 Liberty Drive
Bloomington, IN 47403 USA
www.authorhouse.co.uk
UK TFN: 0800 0148641 (Toll Free inside the UK)
UK Local: 02036 956322 (+44 20 3695 6322 from outside the UK)

Because of the dynamic nature of the Internet, any web addresses or links contained in this book may have changed
since publication and may no longer be valid. The views expressed in this work are solely those of the author and
do not necessarily reflect the views of the publisher, and the publisher hereby disclaims any responsibility for them.

Any people depicted in stock imagery provided by Getty Images are models,
and such images are being used for illustrative purposes only.
Certain stock imagery © Getty Images.

This book is printed on acid-free paper.

ISBN: 978-1-7283-7540-3 (sc)
ISBN: 978-1-7283-7539-7 (e)

Print information available on the last page.

Published by AuthorHouse   09/21/2022

authorHOUSE®

Preface

This is something that I made up for my grandson Levi who was 3 years old at the time, now 8 years old. The Blanket however was a Blanket that belonged to Rupert another grandson of mine aged 6 now.

It's about a blanket that I use to help Levi make things better when he would hurt himself, as at 3 years old he was quite clumsy, and still is, so this was a way to try and help him take his mind off whatever he hurt.

Thanks to Levi my second eldest grandson.

Once there was a little boy named Levi, he was 3 years old and was quite clumsy.

One day his nana came to visit, ",Nana, Nana" Levi shouted as his nana came in the door, he ran up to her to give her a big hug, he tripped over his toy dinosaur that he had left on the floor and landed with a bump on his knees.

"Ouch" cried Levi, "I've hurt my knees Nana" "Oh you are a silly Billy," you shouldn't leave your toys on the floor "said nana, she bent down and reached into her bag and pulled out a blanket, it was blue with white stars on it, she wrap it around Levi's knees and as she rubbed she said this rhyme.

"MAGIC BLANKET, MAGIC BLANKET TAKE AWAY THE PAIN, MAGIC BLANKET MAGIC BLANKET MAKE HIM WELL AGAIN".

4

And as if by magic, Levi began to smile, "is that better" Nana asked," yes, thank you nana" Levi said.

The next time nana came to visit they were playing at building a big tower with Levi's wooden building bricks, when all of a sudden the tower toppled and in his excitement Levi jumped up in the air with a "yippee" and landed on one of the bricks and hurt his foot.

"Ouch" cried Levi "I have hurt my foot nana, "Oh you are a silly Billy " said nana, "you shouldn't jump up and down when there are bricks all over the floor", She then reached into her bag and took out her blanket she wrapped it around Levi's foot and as she rubbed she said this rhyme.

"MAGIC BLANKET MAGIC BLANKET TAKE AWAY THE PAIN, MAGIC BLANKET MAGIC BLANKET MAKE HIM WELL AGAIN".

And as if by magic, Levi began to smile "is that better" nana asked "yes, thank you nana" Levi said.

The next time nana came to visit, they were playing with Levi's train set, Levi laid the track all around the front room, under the coffee table and around the sofa.

"Choo choo" Levi shouted as he ran alongside the train, he ran round the front room, crawled under the table and BUMP, hit his head on the way out.

"Ouch" cried Levi "I've hurt my head nana, "oh you are a silly Billy" said nana, "you should be careful when you are crawling under tables".

She then reached into her bag and took out her blanket, she wrapped it around his head and as she rubbed she said this rhyme.

"MAGIC BLANKET MAGIC BLANKET TAKE AWAY THE PAIN, MAGIC BLANKET MAGIC BLANKET MAKE HIM WELL AGAIN".

12

And as if by magic. Levi began to smile "is that better" nana asked "yes, thank you nana" Levi said.

The next time nana came to visit, they were playing ball in the garden, Levi was kicking the ball back and forth to nana, when he missed a kick and landed on his hands.

"Ouch" cried Levi "I've hurt my hands nana" "Oh you are a silly Billy" said nana, "you should be careful and time your kicks.

She then reached into her bag and took out her blanket, she wrapped it around his hands and as she rubbed she said this rhyme.

"MAGIC BLANKET MAGIC BLANKET TAKE AWAY THE PAIN, MAGIC BLANKET MAGIC BLANKET MAKE HIM WELL AGAIN".

And as if by magic, Levi began to smile "Is that better" nana asked "Yes, thank you nana" Levi said.

The next time nana came to visit, they were playing with Levi's dinosaurs.

"Roar, roar" shouted Levi as he chased after nana.

Nana was pretending to be frightened and ran into the corner of the room, when all of a sudden she tripped over and knocked her knee on the floor.

"Ouch" cried nana "I've hurt my knee Levi" "you are a silly Billy" said Levi "you should be careful when you are running"

Levi knew just what to do, he took the blanket out of nana's bag and wrapped it around her knee and as he rubbed he said this rhyme.

"MAGIC BLANKET MAGIC BLANKET TAKE AWAY THE PAIN, MAGIC BLANKET MAGIC BLANKET MAKE HER WELL AGAIN"

And as if by Magic, nana began to smile "Is that better nana" Levi asked "yes thank you Levi" nana said.

They both began to laugh, they had a big hug.

"Love you nana" Levi said,

"Love you too " nana replied.

The End

Printed in the United States
by Baker & Taylor Publisher Services